Black Bears

(North America and Asian)!

An Animal Encyclopedia for Kids (Bear Kingdom)

Children's Biological Science of Bears Books

PRODIGYWIZARD
BOOKS

HOW ARE NORTH AMERICAN AND ASIAN BLACK BEARS SIMILAR AND DIFFERENT?

Asian black bears are thought to be closely related to the American black bears. Let's find out how.

It is believed these bears came from the same ancestors some four million years ago. They are similar in size, behavior and appearance.

American black bears increased in population, the Asian black bear became endangered due to loss of their habitat. This was caused by several problems like deforestation and hunting.

Asian black bears are said to be more prized than American black bears. They are hunted for their gall bladder which is used in traditional medicine, and they are also a delicacy in some areas.

The most familiar and common bears in North America are the black bears. They live in forests and they climb trees well. But they are also found in swamps and mountains.

Did you know that black bears could be blue-black, brown, cinnamon, blue gray or even white?

DIET

Black bears always love to eat. They eat meat, berries, insects, roots and grasses. They are omnivores. Their diet will vary depending on their location and the season.

BEHAVIOR

Black bears are solitary. They roam large territories. During winter, black bears spend their time in their dens, in caves, burrows and other sheltered spots.

Their body uses the fat which they have built up by eating so much all summer and fall. In mid winter, female black bears give birth to helpless, blind cubs.

If the wind is right, black bears are capable of smelling humans, bears and other animals up to five miles away. Yes, that's quite a distance.

They have a very strong sense of smell which is seven times more powerful than that of a bloodhound. This is because of their extensive nasal structure.

NORTH AMERICAN BLACK BEARS (URSUS AMERICANUS)

These bears are native to North America. They are medium-sized bears and known to be the smallest bear in the continent.

To communicate with other bears, they mark trees using their claws and teeth. This is also common to other species of bear.

American black bears are omnivores. This means that they eat animals, plants like fruit and berries, and insects. They can chase down and kill young deer.

ASIAN BLACK BEAR

This species of bear has a strong sturdy body with a large head and thick legs. Their legs are strong enough to walk and stand using two legs, like people.

Asian black bears have a thick coat of fur, usually black but sometimes brown or blonde. They have a white v-shaped marking on their chest.

Through their long snout, they have a strong sense of smell that will help them in searching for food.

These bears have small claws but they are good climbers and build their nests in the branches, so they can reach for fruit.

They usually eat food high in fat, like walnuts and beechnuts, to build a good fat layer to sustain them through the winter.

Female Asian black bears can have a baby at four or five years old. They usually make babies during the summer months of June and July.

The pregnancy will last for six to eight months. The mother gives birth to up to four hairless cubs in her winter den.

These cubs depend on their mother's warmth and stop drinking their mother's milk when they are six months old.

But even though they are not drinking their mother's milk, the cubs stay with their mother until they are three years old.

Based on the facts given,
what can you say about the two
kinds of bears?

Aren't they lovable?
Do they do their best to
continue their existence in
this unpredictable world?

Maybe humans and bears are somewhat the same in some ways. Think about it.

Made in United States
Orlando, FL
01 May 2023

32673061R00024